IRON MAN
ARMORED ADVENTURES

ATTACK OF THE DRAGON

By Sebastian Belle

Illustrated by Steven E. Gordon

Based on the episode "Tales of Suspense" by Thomas Barichella

Random House 🏠 New York

Copyright © 2011 Marvel Entertainment, LLC, and its subsidiaries. Iron Man: TM & © 2011 Marvel Entertainment, LLC, and its subsidiaries. Animated Series: © 2011 Marvel Entertainment, LLC, and its subsidiaries and Method Films. Nicktoons: TM 2011 Viacom International Inc. All rights reserved. Published in the United States by Random House Children's Books, a division of Random House, Inc., 1745 Broadway, New York, NY 10019, and in Canada by Random House of Canada Limited, Toronto. Random House and the colophon are trademarks of Random House, Inc.

ISBN: 978-0-375-87254-9

www.randomhouse.com/kids

MANUFACTURED IN CHINA   10 9 8 7 6 5 4 3 2 1

3-D special effects by Red Bird Press. All rights reserved.

Teenager Tony Stark was trying to beat the villain known as the Mandarin to the fifth and final Makluan ring. Anyone who wanted these powerful rings had to survive dangerous tests to get them. Unfortunately, the test for the last ring involved a temple with a very, very big dragon named Fin Fang Foom—and Tony didn't have his Iron Man armor with him!

"Hey, ugly! Over here!" Tony yelled, trying to lead the dragon away from his friends Pepper Potts and Gene Khan.

Luckily, Tony's best friend, Rhodey, was wearing the powerful War Machine armor. He smashed through the temple wall and tossed Tony the backpack that held the Iron Man armor.

Rhodey used the massive jets of the War Machine armor to slam into the dragon, giving his friend time to suit up.

"What took you so long?" joked Tony as the Iron Man armor snapped into place around his body.

"We have to get Gene and Pepper out of here," said Iron Man as he rocketed into the air. War Machine unleashed a wave of missiles while Iron Man blasted Fin Fang Foom with repulsor rays. But the gigantic dragon was proving to be more than a match for the combined power of their armor. Tony knew that this test called for a sacrifice—but he didn't want that sacrifice to be one of his friends.

Meanwhile, Gene was shocked to learn that Tony was Iron Man—
because Gene was secretly the Mandarin! Gene liked Tony and his friends.
But as the Mandarin, he was determined to get the fifth Makluan ring—
and no one would stand in his way.

Iron Man and War Machine continued to battle Fin Fang Foom.
Suddenly, Iron Man's onboard computer warned: "Makluan energy buildup
in progress!" Iron Man and War Machine used their repulsor beams to shield
themselves, but the dragon's deadly blast was too powerful. Both of them
were sent flying backward!

The dragon turned from them and began to chase Pepper. Gene decided that if a sacrifice had to be made to obtain the ring, then he would be the one to make it. He pushed Pepper out of the way as Fin Fang Foom's massive jaws snapped shut around him!

But as soon as Gene disappeared down the monster's throat,
Fin Fang Foom froze—and transformed into a harmless crystal statue.
"Gene passed the test," a saddened Tony said to Pepper.
"He sacrificed himself to save you."

Suddenly, Gene emerged from the crystal dragon . . .
dressed as the Mandarin! And now he had all five Makluan rings!
He blasted War Machine as if he were swatting a fly.

"What are you doing, Gene?" yelled Iron Man. "This isn't you!"

"You have no idea who I am," replied the Mandarin. Iron Man and War Machine began to trade blast after blast with the villain. The Mandarin wielded the awesome power of the five rings, but the two heroes were able to repel his every attack.

Just when Iron Man was about to defeat the villain, the Mandarin
used his teleporter ring to disappear.

Tony vowed that no matter how long it took, he would find Gene—